The Rescue Princesses

The Wishing Pearl

More amazing
animal adventures!

The Secret Promise

The Moonlight Mystery

The Stolen Crystals

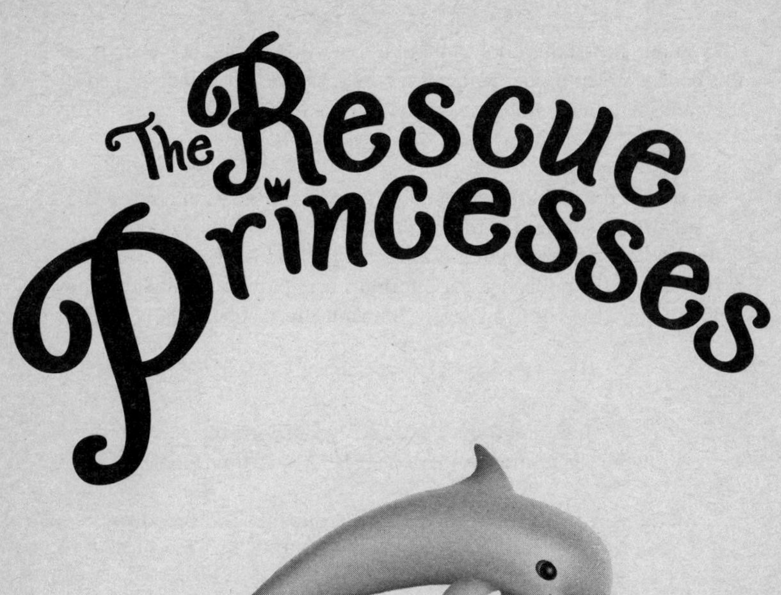

The Wishing Pearl

PAULA HARRISON

Scholastic Inc.

ISBN 978-0-545-50914-5

12 11 10 9 8 7 6 5 4 3 2 1 13 14 15 16 17 18/0

Printed in the U.S.A. 40

First printing, June 2013

To James, thanks for
understanding

CHAPTER ONE

The Island of Ampali

Princess Clarabel scattered the last of her breakfast crumbs for the brightly colored birds that fluttered down to the veranda.

One small blue parrot sat on the wooden railing, eyeing her beadily.

"Go ahead, or there'll be none left." Clarabel laughed, and the little parrot hopped down to peck at the pieces of apricot bread as if he knew exactly what she was saying.

After one last sip of peach juice, Clarabel stepped off the veranda of the white palace onto a lawn that swept down to a clear turquoise ocean.

Her golden hair flew out behind her in the sea breeze and the sapphire ring on her finger sparkled in the sunshine.

She loved staying here on the tropical island of Ampali. It was so much warmer than her home in the kingdom of Winteria, where snow lay on the ground for most of the year.

The little blue parrot flew up to perch on her shoulder.

"Finished breakfast already?" asked Clarabel.

"Squawk!" went the parrot.

Clarabel laughed and turned her eyes back to the ocean. In the distance, a row of small ships with snowy sails was practicing for the Royal Regatta, which was happening in two days' time.

The regatta was a sailboat race and all twenty royal families from around the world had been invited to take part. Clarabel knew her father, the king of Winteria, was down at the harbor right now watching his crew sail.

Quick footsteps sounded behind her. Three princesses came racing out of the white-walled palace, laughing as they ran. Their light summer dresses seemed to float around them.

Princess Emily had red hair and a ruby ring, Jaminta had smooth dark hair and an emerald ring, and Lulu's hair was wavy and black and she wore a ring of yellow topaz.

Clarabel's heart lifted as they came closer. She'd met them all at a Grand Ball in the springtime. They had worked

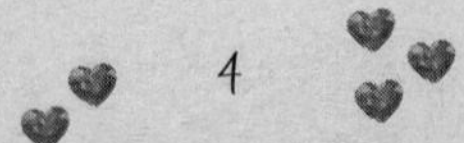

as a team to save the deer of Mistberg Forest and had become close friends at the same time. The best thing about coming to Ampali Island was seeing one another again.

"Run, Clarabel, run!" cried Lulu, her eyes sparkling.

The little blue parrot squawked and flew off Clarabel's shoulder in alarm.

Emily grabbed Clarabel's hand and whirled her away to hide behind a row of palm trees that lined the edge of the garden.

"What's going on?" asked Clarabel, trying to catch her breath.

Emily covered her mouth to stop her giggles, her red curls falling around her face.

"We're making sure Prince Samuel doesn't see us," said Jaminta. "Queen Trudy decided that we should knit some kind of teapot covers for the Royal Regatta, so she sent him to find us and tell us to come inside."

"Teapot covers?" said Clarabel, astonished. "You must mean tea cozies. We're supposed to be making the flower garlands, aren't we?"

"I think Queen Trudy just wants to keep us from having any fun," whispered Emily. "I don't mind making the flower garlands because those will look great on the marquee, but there's no way I'm knitting those teapot things."

"I bet she wants to make us sit still all day. That's what she thinks princesses should do," said Lulu.

"Shh! Here comes Samuel," hissed Jaminta. "Remember your ninja moves, everyone."

The four princesses ducked down. Clarabel silently went through her ninja

training in her mind. Blend in with your surroundings. Wait for the right time to move. The princesses had practiced a few ninja moves in the springtime, but there was so much more to learn.

A scrawny boy with a sulky expression stepped down off the veranda. "I can't see them, Mother," he called back. "They're gone."

Slyly, he looked around him before taking a piece of paper out of his pocket. He unfolded it and held it up to the sunlight. Even from a distance, the paper looked old and frayed at the edges.

With a loud rustling of feathers and leaves, the little blue parrot landed on the palm tree right above Clarabel's head and looked down at her.

"Don't parrots know any ninja moves?" whispered Emily, making Clarabel giggle.

Prince Samuel put the paper back in

his pocket and stared hard in their direction.

The princesses froze as he came closer, peering behind red-flowered bushes. Any minute he would reach the path that led to the palm trees and the princesses' hiding place.

"We have to get to the garden gate," murmured Clarabel.

The others nodded. With slow, silent steps, they crept past the palm trees and down the slope to the end of the garden. When Prince Samuel's back was turned, they opened the gate and slipped through. Ahead of them lay the rolling sand dunes and then the wide blue ocean.

Clarabel shut the gate softly and glanced back. Samuel was walking around the palm trees where they'd been hiding. He was bending down to look into the bushes.

Suddenly, the little blue parrot swooped down from the tree above, squawked loudly in Samuel's ear, and flew away again.

Prince Samuel clutched his head and bolted for the palace as if a gigantic animal were after him.

"Maybe that parrot does know some ninja moves after all," said Clarabel, and they dashed across the sand dunes, filling the air with laughter.

CHAPTER TWO

Princess Training

The princesses ran along the water's edge, the sand flying beneath their feet.

Behind them lay the island's harbor, with long rows of fishing boats and royal sailing ships. Miles and miles of golden beach stretched out in front of them.

"I still can't believe Prince Samuel was scared of a parrot," said Lulu.

"He doesn't seem to like animals very much," replied Clarabel.

"We can't escape him and Queen Trudy forever," said Jaminta. "But let's not go back right away."

"I know what we can do," called Emily, running ahead. "Follow me!"

Emily led them away from the ocean, up the hill by the side of the white palace, and into the rain forest. They stopped in a forest clearing, the chattering of birds and insects all around them.

Emily searched the ground and picked up a long coil of rope lying at the bottom of a tree. "Ally gave me this rope for practicing, so I hid it here. She said if we were serious about rescuing animals, we needed to work on our skills."

Ally was Emily's maid and the princesses trusted her completely. She'd helped them learn ninja skills when they'd rescued a deer during the spring.

"The rope's a great idea," said Lulu. "We can use it to try out some new moves and stuff."

"You mean we should try some climbing and somersaults? Like the drawings you put in all your letters?" asked Clarabel.

Lulu nodded. "I've been practicing acrobatics a lot at home. We need to be ready for anything. One day we might need to rescue a creature at the top of a steep cliff or down a deep hole."

Clarabel stifled a little shiver. When they'd rescued the deer, the princesses had made a secret promise that they would always help an animal in trouble, no matter how dangerous it was. Clarabel didn't really like being up high. But how could she say that when the other princesses didn't seem worried at all?

They had been writing one another letters for weeks discussing what they

needed to practice in order to become good at performing rescues.

Each of the princesses had been at home: Clarabel in the cold land of Winteria, Emily in her leafy kingdom of Middingland, Lulu in the hot country of Undala, and Jaminta in the kingdom of Onica, next to the Silver River.

They had been at opposite corners of the world, but none of them had wanted to forget one another. So they had written letters almost every day.

"This branch will be strong enough." Lulu climbed up the tree and tied the rope firmly halfway along a thick branch. "Who wants to go first?"

"You want to!" said Emily. "Go ahead. Show us what you can do."

Lulu grinned and grabbed the rope. She swung high from the branch, bending her legs backward and forward. With one

final swing she flipped head over heels and landed easily on the soft forest floor.

Jaminta climbed up next and managed several swings. Emily took the next turn, clutching on to the rope and landing safely on the earth.

"I can't do the somersault yet," said Emily breathlessly. "But maybe I will after some practice. Are you ready, Clarabel?"

Clarabel climbed slowly up to the branch and grabbed the rope. Butterflies fluttered inside her. The ground looked so far away — but she had to do this. All the other princesses had.

"Go, Clarabel!" cheered Lulu.

Clarabel took a deep breath and swung free. The earth below rocked scarily. She let herself sway for a few seconds, then dropped to the ground and fell over.

Emily helped her up. "Are you all right?"

Clarabel flushed. "Yes, thanks. I just lost my balance."

"Maybe we should all practice balancing," said Jaminta. "It could be useful in all kinds of different rescues."

"Great idea!" said Lulu. "I saw a fallen tree over this way that would work really well. Let's see if we can find it."

They walked through the forest, hunting for the fallen tree. The rustlings of the rain forest grew louder and Clarabel found herself listening to the animals' calls. She could even hear the chatter of monkeys as they quarreled in the treetops.

"We should test our rings again later on," said Jaminta, shaking her dark hair out of her eyes. "Just to make sure they're still working."

"They've worked really well so far," said Clarabel. "You made them perfectly."

She looked down at the heart-shaped sapphire ring that sparkled on her finger. The other princesses had rings with their own magical jewels, too.

Even though they looked like ordinary rings, these magical jewels enabled the princesses to call one another for help.

Jaminta had invented them. She was very good at shaping precious stones and had learned the craft at home in the kingdom of Onica. By shaping jewels carefully, she could give them special powers.

"Here it is!" said Lulu, stopping next to a large fallen tree. "Who wants to start?"

Clarabel took a deep breath for the second time. "I'll go," she said, climbing up onto the trunk.

She took a few careful steps, trying not to wobble. But the log was slippery and she fell, landing on her hands and knees again.

She scrambled up and tried to smile, but her legs felt shaky.

"Don't worry!" said Emily, seeing her gloomy look. "I think we all need more practice."

Clarabel thanked her, but her blue eyes clouded over. She wasn't hurt, but there was a sinking feeling in her stomach all the same.

Did Emily really think everyone needed more practice, or just her? After all, she was the only one who kept falling over.

Would she ever get better at climbing and acrobatics? If she didn't, was she really good enough to be a Rescue Princess?

CHAPTER THREE

The Turquoise Lagoon

The princesses returned to the palace to find lunch being served in the courtyard.

Rows of white arches stretched along each wall. A beautiful fountain stood in the center, sending arcs of water flying up in the air. The lemon trees were full of fruit. Vases of yellow hibiscus flowers decorated the tables and filled the air with a wonderful scent.

Clarabel gasped to see the huge array of food. Lunch was going to be followed by slices of fresh pineapple and coconut, and lots and lots of ice cream.

The princesses helped themselves and sat down as far away as possible from the frowning Queen Trudy.

"Do you think Queen Trudy knitted the teapot things without us?" whispered Clarabel.

"I don't know, but she doesn't look very happy," replied Emily.

The fair-haired queen of Winteria came by to say hello. "Don't get too hot in the midday sun, girls," she warned with a gentle smile.

"We won't, Mom," said Clarabel.

Then Empress Tia, ruler of Ampali and the other Marica Isles, bustled in with a jug of icy lemonade. Many more kings and queens began to arrive.

The princesses recognized some boys they'd met in the spring — Prince Olaf,

Prince Dinesh, and Prince George — so they gave them a friendly wave.

Prince Olaf came over. "I thought you might like the ice-cream toppings." He handed them a dish of chocolate sauce and some gumdrops.

"Thanks!" said Clarabel, remembering how they'd all liked Olaf before, with his spiky blond hair and big grin.

"My dears!" Empress Tia swept up to them, her coral necklace dangling elegantly below her straight black hair. "I have some jobs for you to do this afternoon. I hope you don't mind."

"Of course not, Your Majesty," said the princesses, each standing up to curtsy.

"Excellent!" The empress's eyes flashed. "I need three of you to help the younger princes and princesses pick flowers to make the garlands. Princesses Emily,

Lulu, and Jaminta, would you like to do that?"

"We'd love to, Your Majesty," replied Emily.

"So that leaves you, Princess Clarabel. I think you'd be good at finding the seashells we need for table decorations. Look for the largest, most beautiful ones you can find. Can you do that?"

"Yes, Your Majesty," said Clarabel, smiling.

"Wonderful!" The empress beamed. "We'll make this the best Royal Regatta yet!"

After lunch, Clarabel skipped out of the palace garden. She turned away from the harbor with its crowd of boats and ran down the golden beach to the ocean.

Waves swished gently up onto the sand and flocks of seabirds circled overhead.

Clarabel scoured the line on the sand where the high tide had reached the previous night. She knew that was where the best shells were often found.

Already she'd picked up five big conch shells and put them in her basket. She was pleased that the empress had asked her to find them.

Glancing at the ocean, she wondered what sea creatures could be playing underneath the waves. Maybe later she'd ask the other princesses to come for a swim.

Clarabel loved swimming. She only wished she was just as good at other things as well.

She spotted another conch shell, picked it up, and dusted the sand off it. Holding it up to one ear, she listened to the restless rushing of the sea inside. It was amazing how such a strong sound could fit inside such a little shell.

Suddenly, there was another sound. A long, low squeaking startled Clarabel. It pulled at her heart like a sad song. She hurried up the beach toward it.

Reaching the top of the sand dunes, she found herself looking down at a wide lake with water as still as glass.

Clarabel had never been this far across Ampali Island before, but the empress had told them about a saltwater lagoon that was only connected to the sea at high tide. She had made the lagoon and most of the seashore into a wildlife zone where all creatures would be safe from harm.

Tall sand dunes stretched along the edge of the lagoon, like giant arms curving around to keep out danger.

The calm turquoise water looked so beautiful. It made Clarabel wish she had her bathing suit on so that she could dive right in.

But then the sound came again, low and piercing this time.

Clarabel rushed over to the edge of the lagoon, put down her basket of shells, and scanned the water for creatures. What could be making a noise so strong and so sad?

At first it was hard to see. The light bounced off the water and dazzled her eyes. Was there something making the surface ripple?

The something moved. It had beady eyes and a mouth curved into a gentle smile. It let out a low squeak and Clarabel gasped.

It was a small gray dolphin with a great gash that stretched from flipper to tail.

No longer thinking about bathing suits, Clarabel dived right into the warm water.

Bubbles streamed past her face as she swam up to the surface and took a gulp of air. Her loose summer dress floated around her in the water. All she could think of was the dolphin and how he seemed to need her.

She swam out farther, but the dolphin had disappeared. Then a gray nose nudged her shoulder. Putting out a hand, she felt smooth, silky skin pass beneath her fingers. She gave a shiver of delight.

This was almost too good to be true. She'd only seen dolphins in pictures before, and now here she was, swimming with one.

"Hello, friend!" she said softly as he glided past her.

The dolphin clicked and squeaked, his black eyes shining. Then he gave a swish of his tail, flicking up drops of water that glittered like a rainbow.

Clarabel pushed her feet off the bottom and paddled alongside him. Then she caught sight of the gash on his side again.

Now that she could see it more clearly, she realized what a deep cut it was. It would probably take a long time to heal.

"Poor thing! What happened to you?" she asked. "Are you all alone here?"

But the dolphin couldn't tell her. Tired now, he stopped swimming completely and his tail flopped in the water. He made a low, sad whistle, as if he was trying to tell her how sick he felt.

"I'll bring you some fish," promised Clarabel. "Maybe that's what you need to get your strength back. You'll be safe here in Ampali's wildlife zone."

She turned and swam back toward the bank. But just as she reached the shallows, she felt another nudge. Twisting around, she saw the dolphin diving down next to her.

Following his movement, she caught a glimpse of something shining beneath the water. He returned, then dived down again as if he wanted Clarabel to follow.

She plunged her face into the clear water, diving side by side with the dolphin. There, on the sandy bed of the lagoon, was a pure-white gem.

Clarabel put out one hand, grasped the sphere between her fingers, and shot to the surface again.

The dolphin bobbed up next to her.

"You found a pearl," said Clarabel, admiring the perfect white gem. "Thank you."

The dolphin clicked and squeaked.

Clarabel waded to the bank. "I'll bring you those fish to help you get better," she called back.

Picking up her basket of shells, she climbed back up the sand dunes. The tropical sun began to dry her summer dress and golden hair.

Clarabel opened her hand to look at the smooth pearl. It glowed white with the tiniest gleam of a rainbow. She couldn't wait to show it to the other princesses. It was beautiful, and the fact that a dolphin had found it for her made it even more precious.

CHAPTER FOUR

Queen Trudy

Clarabel hurried down the sand dunes and back along the beach.

The white palace with its square turrets loomed up ahead of her. It was so different from her castle in Winteria, which had thin, pointed towers jutting up into the sky.

Rushing along, she tripped over a small figure crouching down next to a rock. She lost her balance and fell sprawling onto the sand.

Picking herself up, she tried to shake the sand off her dress just as the figure hid something behind his back.

"Oh, it's you!" Clarabel said, recognizing Prince Samuel, who was looking sulkier than ever.

"Go away!" said Samuel.

But Clarabel had already seen what he was hiding, a metal shovel much too big for making sand castles.

"What are you doing?" she asked, peering around him to look into the large hole he'd made in the sand.

"None of your business!" Samuel cried, his face reddening. "The Nosy Princesses, that's what I'm going to call you and your friends."

But Clarabel wasn't listening. She leaned over the hole. Right in the very bottom rested a whole clutch of smooth white eggs.

"Those are turtle eggs!" She gasped. "You can't dig them up. This is part of the wildlife zone. These creatures are protected."

"Who's going to stop me?" sneered Samuel. "Not you! You spend all your time falling over."

"At least I care about the creatures around me," said Clarabel sharply.

Turning away so that Samuel couldn't see what she was doing, she brought her hand to her lips and pressed the sapphire in the center of her ring.

"Calling all princesses. This is Clarabel speaking. Urgent message: Come down to the beach right now," she whispered, speaking straight into the jewel.

The sapphire glowed deep blue for a second. Then Jaminta's voice came through. "We hear you, Clarabel. We're on our way."

Clarabel turned back to Prince Samuel, who stood by his hole like a puppy guarding a bone. A rolled-up piece of paper poked out from his pocket. He patted it now and then as if he was checking to make sure it was still there. His face glowered as the three other princesses came dashing down the beach toward him.

They arrived, breathless, their faces flushed.

"How did we do?" panted Lulu.

Jaminta checked her watch. "Two and a half minutes. Great practice, everyone."

"Thanks for calling us, Clarabel," said Emily. "We'd just finished the flower garlands."

"This isn't a practice," Clarabel told them. "Just look at what Samuel's digging up."

Emily, Jaminta, and Lulu peered into the hole.

"Turtle eggs!" cried Emily. "You can't dig those up. They might die."

Samuel pouted. "I don't care about the turtles and I don't care about the eggs. I don't want them, anyway. But you can't stop me from digging here."

Clarabel put her hands on her hips. "There are four of us now, so we'll get you out of the way. We can each lift an arm or a leg. Ready, princesses?" She stared at Samuel, her blue eyes unblinking.

Prince Samuel groaned in annoyance. "How did you three get here so quickly, anyway?"

"Wouldn't you like to know," said Lulu, smoothing back her curls.

Samuel cast one more look into the hole, picked up his shovel, and flounced away up the beach.

The princesses quickly began to cover the eggs with sand.

"I told him this was the wildlife zone, but he wouldn't listen," said Clarabel. "He doesn't care about anything except himself."

"I bet he'll go back and tell his mom we were mean to him," said Lulu.

"I think he's up to something," said Clarabel. "He said he wasn't interested in those turtle eggs and he looked like he really meant it. So why was he digging a hole?"

Jaminta's brown eyes turned thoughtful. "If he's hiding something, then we need to find out what it is."

An idea sparked in Clarabel's head. "I've got some binoculars in my suitcase. They could be useful for seeing what Samuel is up to. Let's go get them from my room."

Having carefully covered up all the eggs, the princesses scrambled over the sand dunes and through the back gate to the palace garden. As they ran across the sloping lawn, Clarabel got tired and fell behind the other princesses.

"Hurry up, Clarabel," called Emily, urging her on.

"I'm trying," panted Clarabel, her legs aching.

She clutched the round pearl in her hand. She could hardly wait to tell the others about the dolphin and how he'd found the pearl for her, but she wanted to save it until they were upstairs in private.

They stopped at the door and brushed the sand off their bright summer dresses. Then they tiptoed through the wide hallway, its floor decorated with a beautiful ocean mosaic.

They reached the bottom of the grand staircase just as Queen Trudy of Leepland came down it. The princesses all curtsied to her, just as they'd been taught to do for every king and queen.

"Where did you all go after breakfast?" snapped Queen Trudy. "I needed you to knit some special tea cozies for the royal teapots."

"Sorry, Your Majesty!" Emily curtsied deeply to hide her smile.

The queen sniffed and walked on, before pausing in front of Clarabel and looking her up and down. Her eyes were as hard as stone.

"Princess Clarabel, you look disgraceful!" She stared down a nose so sharp you could have sliced cheese with it. "I hear you've been pestering my poor Samuel, upsetting him while he was quietly playing on the beach. Princesses! You're more like noisy animals!"

"We were trying to stop him from digging up turtle eggs," protested Lulu.

"He was in the wildlife zone," Clarabel added.

"Nonsense!" snapped Queen Trudy. "My Samuel would never do such a thing. And just look at your hair and your clothes, Clarabel. You have clearly been doing something very unbecoming for a princess."

"Mother?" came a whiny voice from above, and Prince Samuel came down the grand staircase dressed neatly in a shirt, matching pants, and an orange vest. He looked like he was ready for a banquet. There wasn't a single speck of sand on him anywhere.

"You see!" Queen Trudy burst out. "Samuel's completely clean, unlike you girls. I will be keeping an eye on all of you from now on, and checking for inappropriate princess behavior!"

She swept out into the courtyard with her nose held high.

Prince Samuel followed his mom with a smirk.

"He's definitely up to something," said Clarabel, pushing back her tangled blond hair.

"It can't be anything good," agreed Lulu.

"We have to find out what it is," said Jaminta. "Maybe we should search his room later. But let's make sure he's out of the way first."

"We'll have to get in and out of there without anyone seeing us," said Emily, her eyes lighting up.

Clarabel grinned. "Fantastic! We can use ninja moves. I was hoping we could do that again!"

CHAPTER FIVE

Clarabel's Pearl

The princesses hurried up to Clarabel's bedroom. A huge four-poster bed filled one corner of the room and wispy curtains flapped in the breeze from the arched windows.

Clarabel rummaged in her suitcase and pulled out light-blue binoculars decorated with the royal crest of Winteria, which featured an Arctic fox.

"Should we check Samuel's room right now?" suggested Emily, glancing through the window. "I can see him down in the courtyard, so his room must be empty."

"Wait!" Clarabel said. "I have something amazing to tell you."

She showed them the pearl, gleaming white with the tiny hint of a rainbow. It was just as beautiful now as when the dolphin had found it for her.

Emily, Lulu, and Jaminta crowded around for a closer look.

"Wow! You don't get many pearls as perfect as that," said Jaminta.

"It all happened when I was looking for seashells." Clarabel's blue eyes shone. "I heard a sound calling me and I followed it. There's a lagoon behind the sand dunes. I swam with a dolphin there and he found this pearl for me."

"You mean that gem came from the bottom of a lagoon?" said Lulu.

"Yes, the dolphin showed me where it was," replied Clarabel.

There was a knock on the door and Emily's maid, Ally, came in. "I brought you something to eat, Your Majesties."

She set a tray down on the table with a jug of pink lemonade and a plate of brownies. Then she began tidying up Clarabel's clothes.

"Thank you, Ally," said the princesses.

Jaminta picked up the gem to have a closer look. "It's such a great pearl," she said, pulling a little jewelry cloth out of her pocket and giving it a polish.

"But there's a sad part." Clarabel's face fell. "The dolphin had a deep cut on his side and he seemed very weak. I promised him I would take him some fish to help him build up his strength."

"You make it sound like he talked to you," said Lulu.

"I think he really understood me," explained Clarabel. "Just from the way he looked and the noises he made."

"I've always wanted to meet a dolphin," said Emily, pushing back her red curls. "I've read that they're really smart creatures. I wonder how he got hurt, though. Did you say the cut was on his side?"

Clarabel nodded. "I'm worried that it won't heal very quickly."

Ally put down Clarabel's clothes and cleared her throat. "It could be that the dolphin was struck by a boat, maybe by a speedboat that was going too fast. That's why the empress doesn't like having speedboats near the island."

"The poor thing!" cried Clarabel.

"At least the dolphin's safe in the wildlife zone now," said Jaminta.

"Let's search Samuel's room first

and then take some fish over to the dolphin," said Emily, helping herself to a brownie.

"Be careful," warned Ally, not looking at all surprised that the girls were planning to search a prince's room. "Queen Trudy is in an extremely bad mood today. If she catches you in her son's room, she'll go straight to the empress and all the kings and queens. Maybe one of you should act as a lookout in case someone comes."

The princesses looked thoughtful. They trusted Ally's advice. Her previous job had been as an undercover agent and she had never forgotten her training.

"I'll be the lookout," said Emily. "Then if anyone comes along I'll keep them talking."

"What other ninja advice can you give us, Ally?" asked Clarabel.

"Well, you should always have an escape route planned, in case you have to leave in a hurry," said Ally.

"Okay then, we'll use Emily as our lookout and have an escape route planned," said Lulu, hopping up and down. "Come on! Let's go!"

Clarabel bit her lip. She wanted to spend a few more minutes planning what to do, but she felt like she was always slowing the others down.

She stashed the dolphin's pearl carefully away in her jewelry box. She was glad that they were going to find out what Samuel was up to, especially if that meant protecting the wildlife zone.

The princesses met at the end of the hallway after they had changed out of their dresses into white T-shirts and leggings that would blend in with the palace walls.

There was a list of all the guests' room numbers in the entrance hall, and with great excitement Clarabel had sneaked downstairs and looked up Samuel's. A pair of blue binoculars hung around her neck, just in case they needed it.

They were going to have to climb two staircases and cross three hallways unseen to reach Samuel's room. They had reached the top of the first staircase when they heard voices close by.

Hiding behind a tall fig plant, they waited until the king and queen of Finia had walked past.

They crept up the next staircase, keeping to the inside of every step. That way they wouldn't be seen by people looking up from the hallway below.

Tiptoeing along the hallways, they stopped at every corner to make sure that no one was walking toward them. Lulu

even performed a series of forward rolls, one after the other, to keep low past a balcony.

Clarabel hurried along, trying her best to keep up with the other princesses. She crept low but didn't dare attempt any acrobatics.

"It's better if we're never even seen up here," whispered Emily. "We don't want Samuel to realize we're checking up on him."

"Number 527. This is Samuel's room," said Jaminta.

Clarabel put her ear against the door. "There's no sound inside. Are we ready?"

The others nodded.

With a shaky hand, Clarabel pushed down the handle. The door opened with a loud creak, making the princesses frown.

Holding her breath, Clarabel made

herself step through the doorway and only breathed out again when she found the place empty.

She scanned the room, noticing a sofa, two chests of drawers, a desk, and a large cupboard set into the wall.

"Check everything," she said quietly, "because we have no idea what we're really looking for."

She pulled open a drawer and quickly shut it again, finding it was only full of orange pants.

Jaminta began checking the other drawers. Lulu set to work on the desk, throwing stuff over her shoulders wildly.

"Lulu, stop!" cried Clarabel.

Lulu looked up in surprise from where she was surrounded by a snowdrift of paper. "What's the matter?" she asked.

"It's so neat and tidy in here," said Clarabel. "If we don't leave everything in exactly the same place, he's sure to notice and suspect someone's been in here."

"Don't worry, I can clean it up," said Lulu, cramming paper back into the desk at high speed.

Clarabel shook back her blond hair and pulled open the next drawer. *This is all T-shirts,* she thought. *We're getting nowhere.* Then something caught her eye.

It was an edge of yellowy paper, half hidden by a box of tissues. Gently, she pulled the paper out. It curled up into a tube shape and she had to unroll it on the floor to see the writing.

"Lulu! Jaminta! Come and look at this," she said.

They all leaned over the old sheet of paper, looking at its strange inky markings.

Suddenly, footsteps sounded nearby and the princesses froze. Someone

coughed, and it sounded as if they were right inside the closet.

The girls stared at one another in panic. Emily, as the lookout, hadn't warned them of anything. So what was going on?

Another cough came from the closet, and with a sudden shock Clarabel realized the truth. The closet wasn't a closet at all. It was the doorway through to the bedroom next door.

And someone was in there right now.

CHAPTER SIX

The Rising Gull

The door handle to the next-door room began to bend slowly down.

At lightning speed, the princesses shoved as much as they could back in place. Then they looked for somewhere to hide.

"Here!" hissed Clarabel, diving under the bed.

Lulu and Jaminta dived after her.

The door swung open and a pair of brown high-heeled shoes strutted past the bed, inches from the princesses' noses.

Clarabel tried to keep as still as she possibly could, although with Lulu's feet pressed hard against her ear, it wasn't easy. Focusing on her ninja training, she remembered something Ally had once told them: When you're hiding, imagine you're a part of your hiding place.

Just then, a large black beetle crawled across her hand. Clarabel clamped her mouth shut to stifle a gasp. She didn't like beetles very much, but she didn't dare move.

The insect was so close she could see all its legs and feelers. She kept very still, and luckily the beetle scuttled away.

The brown high-heeled shoes paused next to the chest of drawers and there was a scraping sound of drawers opening.

"So untidy!" muttered a voice. "Samuel must come and clean up his room."

That's Queen Trudy, thought Clarabel, recognizing the voice.

Lulu, who, as the tallest, was the most squashed, shifted her leg and banged it against the underside of the bed. The bedsprings made a loud twanging sound.

The shoes stopped, then walked slowly toward the girls.

Clarabel held her breath and hoped that Lulu and Jaminta were doing the same. The large black beetle had crawled across the floor to the tip of the queen's shoe.

"Ugh! A bug!" cried the queen, twitching her foot out of the way. But the beetle followed her, heading toward the other shoe.

Queen Trudy let out an ear-piercing shriek. Lifting her skirts, she fled out of the room and slammed the door behind her.

The princesses crawled out from under the bed and collapsed into giggles.

"A bug! A bug!" cried Lulu in a high-pitched voice.

"We'd better hurry," said Clarabel, taking a deep breath to stop her laughter. "She might make Samuel come up here right away."

She fished the yellowy paper back out of the drawer and they all bent over it.

"It's really old." Lulu held down the curling edge of the paper. "And the ink's faded. But it's definitely a map."

"It says '*Rising Gull.*' I wonder what that is," said Clarabel.

"We need to remember all of this," said Jaminta. She grabbed a piece of paper from the desk drawer and started copying the map and all the writing.

Clarabel peered out of the window and across the balcony. "Samuel's not in the courtyard anymore. We have to get out of here."

The girls replaced the map back under the tissue box and crept out into the hallway.

Emily, who had been keeping watch outside the door, put a finger to her lips. Voices drifted down the hallway, getting louder and louder.

"It's Samuel and Queen Trudy," hissed Emily.

Clarabel looked around, her heart thumping. The hallway was a dead end. "There's nowhere to go!" she said.

"We forgot to plan an escape route, like Ally told us to," whispered Jaminta. "We rushed up here too fast."

The voices grew louder. The girls crept back into Samuel's room again and looked doubtfully at the bed.

"Not under there again! It's so squashed." Lulu groaned.

Clarabel climbed out onto the balcony. "If we use a chair we can probably reach the roof. Then we can climb down the outside stairs into the garden. I think it's our best hope."

Her stomach felt hollow. She couldn't believe she was actually suggesting climbing up so high.

"Let's do it!" said Lulu, pulling herself up immediately.

Emily and Jaminta followed and Clarabel climbed up last, just as she heard the door handle click.

The roof of the palace was completely flat, surrounded by many square, white turrets. The princesses crept across it and down the spiral steps at one end.

Clarabel held on to the handrail and

tried very hard not to look at the ground. She caught Emily staring at her and her heart sank. She had to try and seem braver than she felt.

When they finally reached the safety of Clarabel's room, the princesses studied the map again.

"The *Rising Gull.* I recognize that name," said Emily. "It was a story that Ally used to tell me when I was little. It was about a treasure ship that sank near an island, and the treasure was supposed to be buried on the island somewhere. The ship's name was the *Rising Gull.* I always thought it was just a story."

"This is a map of Ampali," said Clarabel. "Look — here's the harbor, and here's the lagoon. Maybe this is the island where the ship sank long ago."

"I bet Samuel thinks so. I wonder how he got ahold of the map," said Jaminta.

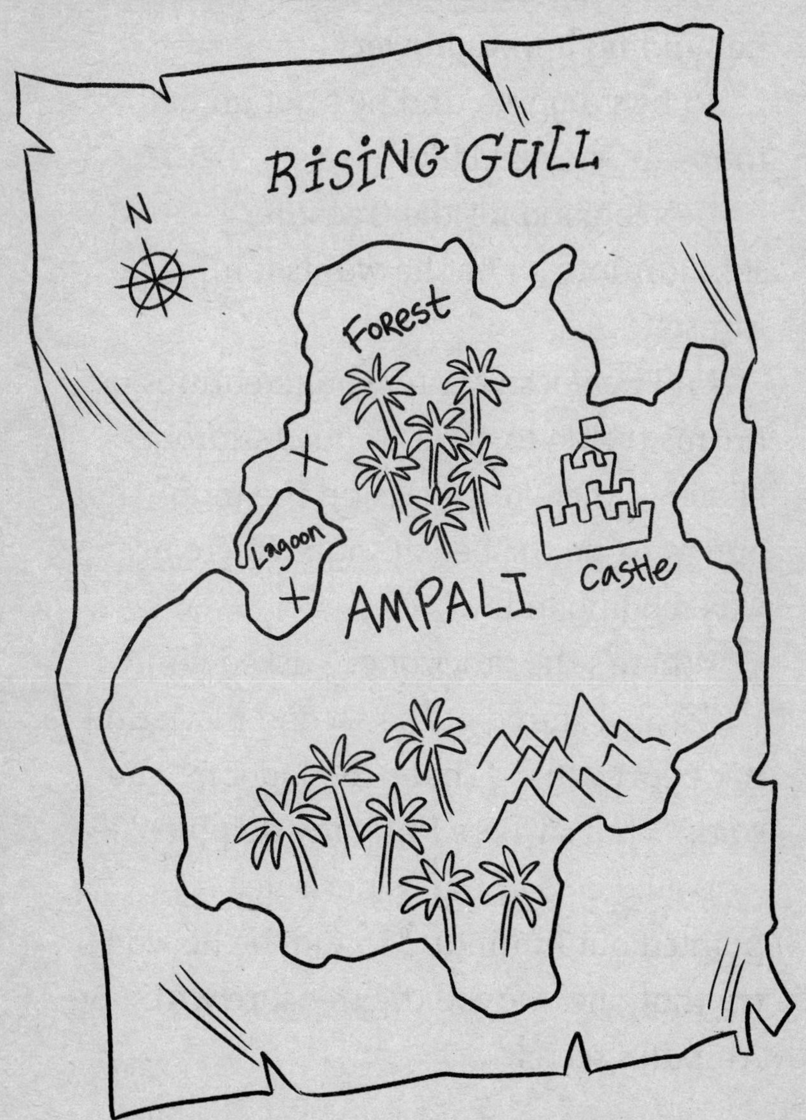
RISING GULL
N
Forest
Lagoon
Castle
AMPALI

"He must not have told Queen Trudy if he's hiding it in a drawer."

"So he's digging and he's got an old map . . ." started Lulu.

"He's looking for the treasure," said Jaminta. "I bet he wants it all for himself."

"And he doesn't care what creatures he harms trying to get it," added Clarabel. "Look — there're two Xs on the map. That one must be the beach, right where he was digging today."

"Where's the other one?" asked Emily.

Clarabel stared at the second mark and her heart sank. "That's the lagoon," she said. "That's where I met my dolphin."

"Well, he can't dig underwater," pointed out Jaminta. "So maybe he won't try that one. Maybe the treasure will stay Ampali's secret."

"It would be cool if we could find it!" said Lulu.

"I hope Samuel doesn't start messing around in the lagoon," said Clarabel. "My dolphin's resting there."

Emily patted her shoulder. "Let's go and ask Cook for that fish. It's time we paid your dolphin a visit."

As the girls bounded down the stairs to the kitchen, Clarabel couldn't help worrying. What if Samuel did want to search for treasure in the lagoon? What would he try to do?

Did he have enough heart to be kind to a hurt dolphin?

CHAPTER SEVEN

Swimming by Moonlight

It was almost dark by the time the princesses had any time to themselves again.

The empress had caught them on the way to the kitchens and insisted on seeing Clarabel's seashells and the completed flower garlands.

"There's so much to do!" she'd said. "It's such a relief that you princesses are willing to help."

Then she'd shown them how to fold

napkins into swan shapes to go on the dinner table that evening.

Clarabel didn't mind helping, but she wished the empress hadn't chosen that moment to ask them. The minutes ticked by, one after another, and then it was time to get ready for dinner.

Clarabel put on a long, flowing dress made from light-blue silk that shimmered in the evening light.

She hung her sapphire necklace around her neck and slipped her feet into gold shoes studded with tiny diamonds.

She thought longingly about the dolphin. Why did everything have to take so long? She was sure he would be waiting for her.

At least she'd managed to hide some fish at the far end of the palace garden. They were there, ready, as soon as the princesses had the chance to slip away.

The princesses walked together to the dinner tables set up on the palace lawn.

Jaminta wore green silk pants and a top with a necklace of sparkling emeralds. Emily had chosen a short pink dress, and a black velvet hairband to pull back her red curls. Lulu, who wanted to stand out, wore a dress of yellow and purple swirls, and a necklace made from dozens of tiny shells.

"Stay away from the wildlife zone," Lulu muttered to Samuel as they passed him on the lawn.

"Please don't dig up any more eggs," added Clarabel.

But Prince Samuel just curled his lip and looked away.

They ate a delicious dinner of roast chicken followed by tall ice-cream sundaes covered with strawberry sauce.

The kings and queens talked endlessly. They discussed the boats entering the Royal Regatta and how well the sailing practice was going. They talked so much that Lulu started drumming her fingers impatiently on the table.

By the time all twenty royal families had finished, the sky had turned a dark blue sprinkled with little stars. Lanterns were lit and a band began to play a jazzy song.

The kings and queens got up to dance and Clarabel smiled to see the younger princes and princesses jumping around with the adults.

Prince Dinesh and Prince George had settled in a corner with a pack of cards. Prince Samuel was nowhere to be seen.

"Where's Samuel?" hissed Lulu. "I don't like not knowing where he is."

"We should go to the lagoon now," murmured Emily. "While they're all too busy to notice we're gone."

Clarabel looked around. She really wanted this to work. If they were caught leaving, she'd never get the dolphin the fish she'd promised him.

Rising from their seats, the girls walked across the lawn chatting, as if they were just going for a stroll. But as soon as they reached the row of palm trees, out of sight of the dancers, they burst into a run.

Clarabel stopped by a yellow hibiscus plant and felt around in the shadows until she found a flat parcel wrapped in brown paper. Even through the paper it had the unmistakable smell of fish.

Prince Olaf passed her carrying a tray of extra napkins. Clarabel put a finger to her lips to show that he should pretend she wasn't there. The prince grinned and walked on.

Smothering their laughter, the princesses left their party shoes under a bush near the gate and leapt over the sand dunes.

A bright full moon rose up out of the ocean just as they reached the water's edge. To the left, they could see the dark outlines of the boats in the harbor.

They ran on, the sand soft under their bare feet. Clarabel led the way, looking for the place where she had crossed the dunes to find the lagoon earlier that day.

Up on the hillside, hundreds of smudges of orange light came from the palace lanterns and the music drifted down toward the ocean.

"It's this way," called Clarabel, speeding up in her excitement. For once, she felt as if she was running pretty fast.

At the crest of the dune, she stopped. The deep-blue lagoon lay before her and the bright moon made a path of light all the way across it.

"How beautiful!" said Emily.

The surface of the water stirred, and a squeaking and clicking noise started.

"That's my dolphin!" cried Clarabel.

The princesses quickly pulled off their dresses. Underneath they had on the bathing suits that they'd secretly been wearing the whole evening.

They ran down to the edge and dived into the warm lagoon. Swimming back up to the surface, they laughed and splashed one another with drops of water turned silver by the moonlight.

Clarabel was the last to get in. She unwrapped the fish from the brown paper and waded over to the dolphin.

The creature squeaked at her, but he moved slowly and his tail drooped in the water.

She pulled off some fish and gave it to him, but he hardly took a bite. Behind the smiling mouth, his eyes looked sad.

"You poor thing!" said Clarabel, stroking his silky gray skin.

The dolphin clicked his reply, staying close to her side.

Jaminta joined them. "That's quite a nasty gash," she said, looking at his side. "Usually dolphins stay together, but this one must have been separated from his friends when the accident happened."

Clarabel's eyes filled with tears. "I thought the fish would help. But he seems too weak even to eat it."

She tried to offer him the fish again. He flapped a flipper limply but didn't seem interested in the food.

Clarabel watched him sadly. "You'll never get better if you can't even eat. What should we do?"

Emily swam over to them. "I asked Ally to find out if there are any vets here. But she said the island is too small to have one."

"It's up to us, then," said Clarabel, her pale face determined. "We'll find a way to cure him."

"I don't know if that's even possible," said Jaminta.

"It has to be!" Clarabel stroked the dolphin's nose. "Look at all the things you can do with the jewels, Jaminta. There has to be a way!"

Suddenly, they noticed Lulu waving her arms frantically at them from the shore.

"What is it?" called Emily.

But Lulu put her finger to her lips and

beckoned to them. So Jaminta and Emily swam swiftly to the water's edge.

Clarabel kissed her dolphin on the nose before she followed the others. "I'll come back soon," she promised. "I'll find a way to make you feel better."

Lulu made them all duck down behind a sand dune. Clarabel froze as she saw why they were hiding. There, on top of the dunes and clearly outlined in the moonlight, was the figure of Prince Samuel.

"He's got his shovel," whispered Lulu.

"He's going to dig for the treasure again," said Jaminta.

They watched Samuel trudge around the edge of the lagoon and disappear over the other side.

"Let's go!" said Lulu, straightening up. "We have to follow him without him seeing us. We have to find out where he's going next."

"But the dolphin —" started Clarabel.

"If Samuel's doing something sneaky, we have to go and see what it is," Lulu insisted, her hands on her hips. "I'll go first. I can stay unseen by keeping low."

Clarabel's shoulders tightened. "But it's just —"

"We have to hurry!" interrupted Lulu.

Clarabel's heart began to race. It felt wrong to be bossy, but she had to make herself do it.

"No!" she said quietly. "We spent all afternoon finding out what Samuel's up to and now that we've finally got here, the dolphin's much worse than before. We have to put him first. He needs us. That was what our Rescue Princesses promise was all about."

Clarabel stopped and took a deep breath. Emily patted her arm sympathetically.

Lulu looked surprised for a moment, but then she smiled. "You're right, Clarabel! This little dolphin is much more important than any prince."

"And Rescue Princesses should stick together," added Emily.

"All right, then, let's get started," said Jaminta.

The princesses picked up their clothes and raced away toward the beach.

Clarabel, the slowest, ran behind, her head filled with the picture of a little dolphin lying still in the deep-blue water.

CHAPTER EIGHT

The Ocean Gem

They sneaked into Jaminta's room half an hour before midnight.

Jaminta took out a polished wooden box, opened it up, and laid out all her jewel-sculpting tools on the table.

Clarabel held the sapphire bracelet she'd collected from her bedroom.

"Have you ever made a jewel that can heal something before?" Clarabel asked her.

Jaminta frowned. "No. I've made

emeralds that light up, diamonds that can detect metal, and the rings that we use to call each other. But none of the jewelry I've made changes a living thing. This is something new."

"If anyone can do it, it's you, Jaminta," said Emily.

"I'm going to try using Clarabel's sapphires because she's the one who knows the dolphin the best." Jaminta took Clarabel's bracelet and gently tapped each jewel in turn with her tiny chisel, chipping them into a circular shape.

"Here's something we can test it on," said Lulu, holding up a wilting potted plant. "I found it by a window in the hallway. It could use some healing."

"If the plant recovers, then so will the dolphin." Clarabel clasped her hands together.

"I hope so," said Jaminta seriously.

Clarabel could feel the seconds ticking by while Jaminta gave each gem a little polish. Finally, after turning the bracelet this way and that to look at all the jewels, she placed the bracelet around the plant's stem.

"Now we wait and see, I guess," said Emily.

So they waited, watching the plant closely. But nothing happened. The leaves remained wilted and slightly brown.

Clarabel's hopeful face fell.

The clock chimed midnight.

"Let's try again in the morning," said Jaminta. "Right now, we need some sleep."

The morning dawned with a gray sky and a blustery wind.

The princesses were up early, before

most of their parents had woken up. Ally brought them a breakfast of cherry muffins and pancakes in the enormous dining room.

The empress walked past with Queen Trudy, who was talking very loudly about Samuel. "He's such a sweet boy, and so smart! He's learning to fish now and has borrowed a net from the harbor fishermen."

Clarabel frowned. Something seemed wrong about what Queen Trudy had just said. But she and the empress left the dining room before Clarabel could hear any more of their conversation.

Ally handed out pancakes and syrup. "Be careful around the island today because there's a tropical storm coming. It was a storm like this that sunk that old ship, the *Rising Gull.*"

"Do you think the treasure from that

ship is still somewhere on the island?" asked Lulu excitedly.

Ally nodded. "I think so. Jewel thieves have been searching for it for years. But no one ever had the map, so no one could find it."

"But we know who has the map! It's Prince Samuel!" whispered Emily, nearly knocking over the syrup.

Ally shook her head. "I think that the treasure really belongs to Ampali Island now, and that's how it should stay." She filled their glasses with strawberry milk. "What were you girls doing up so late last night, anyway?"

"We were trying to craft a jewel that could make the dolphin better," explained Jaminta. "But it didn't work."

"Maybe you need an ocean gem for an ocean creature," said Ally, heading back toward the kitchens.

Clarabel took a sip of strawberry milk, then she put her glass down with a snap. "An ocean gem!" she exclaimed, her face lighting up like the sun. Leaving her cherry muffin behind, she ran to her bedroom, nearly bumping into a bad-tempered Queen Trudy on the way.

Opening her jewelry box, she gently picked up her pearl. Could this be the ocean gem that would heal the dolphin? After all, pearls were made in the sea, inside little shells.

Clarabel put the pearl into her pocket and smiled. Maybe this was the answer. The thought of her dolphin being healthy again made her so happy she felt as if she was glowing.

She hurried down the grand staircase, but something stopped her halfway. A faint noise echoed around her. It made her skin prickle.

It was a high, unhappy sound. Without knowing why, she reached for her pocket and drew out the pearl, which was slightly warm.

The noise came again, and this time she recognized the dolphin's calls coming from the pearl.

The sound wrenched at her heart.

The dolphin was in trouble and he was calling her.

CHAPTER NINE

The Dolphin's Call

Clarabel flew back to the dining room, her golden hair falling over her shoulders.

"We have to go! It's the dolphin!" she said breathlessly to the other princesses, and she held out the pearl.

Emily looked confused. "We figured you were getting the pearl. That could be just what we need. But why do we have to go right now?"

"I can hear him calling. He's in

trouble," said Clarabel desperately. "No time to explain."

"One second," Jaminta said firmly, and, taking the pearl from Clarabel's fingers, she laid it next to the sapphire bracelet from the previous night.

Then, with a swift tap and some careful bending of metal, she took one sapphire out of the bracelet and set the pearl in its place.

"Thanks," said Clarabel as Jaminta handed back the new pearl-and-sapphire bracelet.

"If the dolphin's in trouble, then let's go!" said Lulu.

Dashing out of the palace, they arrived at the beach in record time. They battled strong winds that tried to whisk them off their feet as they crossed the sands. The storm swept closer, its black clouds looming.

"The storm will reach Ampali Island really soon," Jaminta shouted over the noise of the wind.

"I know!" yelled Clarabel. "But I'm not going back until I've helped the dolphin."

She could still hear his sad calls coming through the pearl and it made her run even faster.

As she climbed up the steep dunes, she noticed a pair of footprints already leading that way, and her worry deepened.

Reaching the top of the dunes, she stared down at the lagoon below. Gone was the clear turquoise water. Instead, the lagoon was as gray as the sky, with the surface whipped up into sharp waves.

By the edge stood a drenched Prince Samuel, with an enormous tangled mess of fishing net in his hands.

Clarabel ran down the slope toward

him. "What have you done? Where's the dolphin?"

She scanned the choppy water, but there was no silky gray shape poking its nose above the surface.

"It pulled me in," said Samuel sulkily. "Now I'm all wet."

"The dolphin pulled you in! That doesn't sound right. What were you doing, anyway?" demanded Jaminta, looking at the tangled black net.

"Nothing! Just fishing," said Samuel quickly.

"You were trying to get the treasure using the fishing net!" guessed Lulu. "That's just silly!"

Prince Samuel jumped and turned red, then purple. "I knew you princesses were too nosy. How did you find out about my treasure? I won't let you have any of it!"

"We're not here for the treasure. We're

here to help an injured dolphin," said Clarabel.

Prince Samuel scowled. "Your dolphin spoiled everything, getting in the way of my net." He gave the net a kick and muttered, "All those gold bars and coins must be down there somewhere."

"You mean the dolphin got tangled up in your net?" said Clarabel. "How could you be so mean? He must have been terrified."

Dark storm clouds swept over their heads, covering every bit of blue sky.

Prince Samuel ignored Clarabel and stomped away up the sand dunes, trying to keep his balance in the driving wind.

Clarabel ran after him. "What happened to the dolphin?"

"It swam down there." Prince Samuel glowered at her and pointed toward the mouth of the lagoon.

"I'm not staying out here in a storm," he shouted. Then he left without a backward glance.

Clarabel stared at the tiny channel of water where the lagoon met the sea. Her dolphin was gone.

Emily, Lulu, and Jaminta joined her. The wind howled around them and rain began to beat against their faces.

"Why did he think he'd catch the treasure in a net?" Jaminta wondered aloud. "It's much too heavy."

"He wasn't thinking at all. The poor dolphin!" said Emily, shaking her head.

"He must have gotten tangled up in Samuel's net and been really scared," said Clarabel. "Then he must have swum out of the lagoon into the sea to escape."

She chewed her lip. If only she'd run faster. If only she'd stopped Samuel in time.

Lightning cut through the sky in a jagged flash and thunder boomed. Her dolphin had left the safe lagoon at a terrible time.

The storm had pounced, and the dolphin was out there, somewhere, trying to stay alive.

CHAPTER TEN

Fighting the Storm

Clarabel stared out to sea, rainwater pouring down her face.

The dolphin must be so scared, and with his injury he would be struggling to swim.

He could easily be swept against the sharp rocks that surrounded parts of the island. He never should have left the lagoon.

"I was too late," she said sadly. "I heard

him calling, but I didn't get here fast enough." Tears sprang to her eyes, and she wiped them away.

Lulu put an arm around her shoulder. "Don't worry. We'll go out there and find him."

"We can't take a sailboat out in this wind. We'll get blown straight into rocks," said Jaminta.

"There's a rowboat in the harbor that belongs to my family," said Emily. "We could make that work."

They sprinted along the beach to the harbor while the rain hurled against them. The harbor was empty of people, and all the ships were safely anchored against the storm.

The princesses clambered into the little red rowboat. They untied the rope that fastened it to the harbor wall and pulled the rope inside the boat.

They sat down, two girls to each oar, dipping the oars into the water and pulling in time with one another.

"If I'd known we'd be doing this" — Emily puffed — "I'd have suggested more rowing practice."

Once they passed the safety of the harbor walls, the storm hit them with terrifying force.

The princesses rowed as hard as they could, but the waves were very high. The little boat climbed up each mountain of water and fell straight down the other side.

Clarabel held the bracelet with the pearl close to her ear. "He's still calling me. It's this way." She pointed across the stormy ocean.

The dolphin's call was faint behind the thundering of the waves, but she knew she couldn't let him down.

Rowing west along the coast, the girls fought the rising ocean. Their hair was plastered against their heads by the rain and salt spray.

Clarabel's heart fluttered as she spotted a small gray shape among the plunging waves. "Come here! Follow us!" she cried to him. But the dolphin was too weak to swim and drifted closer and closer to the rocks.

"One of us has to go in and help him to the shore," called Lulu over the rumble of thunder. "I'll do it. I'm strong because of all the extra acrobatics I've been doing."

"Maybe I should do it," said Clarabel. "The dolphin trusts me. He'll follow me."

"Are you sure?" asked Emily. "The waves are so high. Won't you be scared?"

"Do you really want to?" asked Jaminta.

Clarabel swallowed and nodded. "I want to do it. The dolphin needs me."

So Jaminta tied one end of the rope to the bottom of the boat, ready to throw the other end out into the water.

Clarabel's hands shook a little as she fastened her bracelet really tightly around her wrist. She pulled off her dress and stood ready in her bathing suit. With her face pale and her eyes fixed on the dolphin, she dived in.

A mountain of gray water swallowed her up. She reached the surface spluttering and grabbed on to the rope.

She swam right over to the dolphin's side and stroked his silky skin. The dolphin gazed at her, his black eyes frightened.

"Don't worry, we're going back. Stay with me and you'll be safe," said Clarabel softly.

Jaminta, Lulu, and Emily rowed back toward Ampali. They pulled strongly through the water, and this tim[illegible] power of the waves helped the rowbo[illegible] along.

Clarabel held on tightly to the rope and let the boat pull her through the ocean. The sea kept pushing her down and she came up several times gasping for breath.

She tried to be brave, talking to her dolphin and urging him on.

The dolphin managed to swim a little, gathering his strength from Clarabel beside him. He fought wave after towering wave.

At last, the mouth of the lagoon came into view. The palm trees on either side were bent right over in the fierce wind.

The dolphin flopped in the water, unable to swim any more. Clarabel put one arm around his body and held tight, shouting to the princesses to row harder.

A dart of lightning ripped across the

rack of thunder. The
, sending more sheets of
wn.
beat us!" Lulu shouted at
e rowed.

vhispered to the dolphin, telling h[illegible] not to be scared. Even with the noise of the wind and rain, she knew he understood.

As they rowed into the channel that led to the lagoon, the storm let out a great roar, as if it was angry that they'd escaped.

Jaminta, Emily, and Lulu dropped to a slower rowing speed. They passed through the opening in the sandbank, and parrots squawked unseen among the bushes on each side.

"Nearly there!" gasped Clarabel, still holding tightly to the rope.

The dolphin cried softly.

Inside the lagoon, the princesses rested on their oars, trying to get their breath back.

With one final growl, the storm passed on and the rain grew lighter. The lagoon became calm and the water returned to a beautiful turquoise color once again.

The girls slipped out of the boat to join Clarabel in the warm water. They formed a circle around the dolphin, but he lay very still, barely able to lift his nose.

"He's so weak from struggling against the waves," said Clarabel, tears coming to her eyes. "What should we do? He can't even swim."

"We have to try the pearl," said Jaminta. "We haven't had time to test it first. But we have to try it now. It's our only hope for making him better."

CHAPTER ELEVEN

The Wish

Clarabel unfastened her bracelet.

The blue sapphires glittered deeply, and the pearl, with its gleam of a rainbow, cast a bright reflection in the water.

Holding them carefully, she made sure that they were right next to the terrible wound on the dolphin's side. The sapphires and the pearl glowed together in the rhythm of a heartbeat.

"Is it working?" asked Lulu.

"I'm not sure," replied Emily.

"Let's wait another minute," said Jaminta.

The dolphin lay silent. For a moment, nothing in the lagoon moved at all. And still nothing happened.

Clarabel shut her eyes and held her breath. With her whole heart she said, "I wish he could be healthy again, I wish he could be healthy again . . ."

The pearl's rainbow shine grew brighter. A fine white mist floated from the pearl to the dolphin. Under the haze, the dolphin seemed to fill with light.

Clarabel opened her eyes and stared.

"It's the pearl! It's starting to work," she whispered.

The dolphin turned his beady black eyes toward the princesses and nuzzled each one of them with his nose.

"You're better!" cried Clarabel, touching his smooth skin. She could still see where the cut had been, but it was healed over and smooth.

Jaminta looked amazed. "I've never seen a jewel work like this before. I think you made it happen, Clarabel."

"It was like the pearl knew what you were wishing for," said Emily softly.

The dolphin squeaked and thumped his tail. Then, with a wiggle and a splash, he dived away across the lagoon.

"Come on!" called Lulu, and all the princesses dived under. They came to the surface and stood up in the shallow water, looking for the little dolphin.

Suddenly, the water filled with splashes and chirps.

"More dolphins!" said Emily. "The dolphin's friends came back to find him!"

The little dolphin tipped his nose into the air and went leaping and diving with his friends.

Lulu held on to a dolphin's fin and went for a ride. "This is so much fun!"

"I know!" Emily laughed, holding on to another.

"That was a great rescue, girls," said Jaminta, splashing everybody.

Clarabel's heart felt full enough to burst as the dolphin swam back to her again.

"It's great to see you feeling so much better," she said.

The dolphin squeaked and flicked the water with his tail, leading her across the lagoon. Clarabel smiled, a little puzzled. Something told her he wasn't playing anymore.

Halfway across, the dolphin dived down under the water. Then he resurfaced, making his clicking sound again.

"What is it?" Clarabel asked him.

He dived again and she followed, swimming right down to the bottom.

Half hidden in the sand lay a broken wooden chest with gold bars and coins spilling out of it. They filled the water all around with sparkling color. Clarabel's eyes widened and she returned to the surface for a gulp of air.

"You showed me the treasure!" she said. "You knew where it was the whole time."

A silky nose brushed her cheek before the dolphin squeaked and dived away across the lagoon.

"Thank you," said Clarabel. "Good luck, little one."

CHAPTER TWELVE

The Treasure Chest

The following morning, the sun blazed down from a clear blue sky.

Everyone hurried around the palace, making things perfect for the enormous banquet that would follow the Royal Regatta.

Some of the flower garlands needed mending, but other than that the storm had caused very little damage.

The princesses asked for Ally's help to get the treasure out of the lagoon, as the chest was half full of sand and really heavy.

"So that's where the treasure's been hiding all these years!" said Ally as she helped pull it to the shore.

"Was this the most famous lost treasure of all?" asked Emily.

Ally shook her head. "No. The most famous treasure is the Onica Heart Crystals. Those crystals are rarer than diamonds."

"I know about them," said Jaminta, who came from the kingdom of Onica. "They belonged to my grandfather, but they disappeared before I was born."

"What happened to them, Ally?" asked Clarabel. "You must know all about it because of your old job."

"Yes, tell us! Were they lost or stolen?" asked Emily.

"I did work on that case for a while,

but it was all very secret," said Ally mysteriously.

"Please tell us!" the princesses pleaded. But Ally shook her head and wouldn't say any more.

Jaminta rigged up a small wooden cart with wheels and a rope so that they could get the treasure up to the palace. They got stuck on some of the sand dunes, but finally, after a lot of tugging and heaving, they made it into the palace garden.

They arrived just as the empress began to speak to a crowd of all the kings, queens, princes, and princesses who had gathered together on the lawn.

"It gives me great pleasure to declare that this Royal Regatta has begun," announced the empress. "Now, let's walk down to the harbor, where the boat race will start, and—"

She stopped as she took in the strange sight of the princesses wheeling a treasure chest up the sloping lawn.

The empress walked through the crowd to meet them.

"The lost treasure of the *Rising Gull*! My dears, I've been waiting years for someone to uncover it. I should have known it would be you four princesses!"

Her wise eyes moved from one princess to another. "How did you find it?"

"We found it by accident — well, a dolphin helped us, really," Clarabel blurted out.

"How strange!" said the empress. "But, I have always thought that they're very clever creatures. So what do you plan to do with all this gold?"

Clarabel curtsied. "Your Majesty, we would like to give the treasure to you, because we truly believe it belongs to Ampali Island now."

Prince Samuel burst through the crowd with a loud cry but was yanked back by Queen Trudy.

"We think it should be used to support the wildlife zone and all the creatures in it," added Clarabel. "Especially the dolphins."

The crowd broke into cheers and applause, making Clarabel blush. Her parents, the king and queen of Winteria, came to the front.

"What a lovely idea, Clarabel," said her mom, smiling. "We're so proud of you."

"Wow! So that's why you were so busy," said Prince Olaf, looking at the chest full of coins and gold bars.

"Very busy! And you still managed to

make the flower garlands, too!" said the empress.

The four princesses curtsied and the empress smiled. "You must take something from the chest to remember your great achievement," she added.

"But . . . but . . . that's not fair!" whined Samuel, not noticing the sudden silence. "I was looking for it first, so it should be *my* gold."

The empress frowned. "So was it you who took the map from my private bookcase two days ago?"

Prince Samuel flushed. "*I* haven't got a map. Maybe *they* took it." He pointed at the princesses.

All the kings and queens turned to stare at Clarabel, Emily, Lulu, and Jaminta.

"Squawk!" went a little blue parrot landing on Samuel's shoulder. Samuel gave a screech and stumbled backward.

As he fell over onto the lawn, the old map fell out of his pocket and lay there on the grass.

"It *was* you, Prince Samuel," said the empress sternly. "You took the map without asking and then lied about it. We will have to find you a suitable punishment. I know! You will feed and clean up after all the palace pets for the rest of the week."

Samuel pouted and slunk back toward the palace. Queen Trudy followed him, scolding in a whisper.

The empress turned back to Clarabel. "You must take something. I insist!"

Clarabel leaned over the treasure chest. She didn't want any gold — that should be used for the wildlife zone. But there, in one corner, was a gleam of purple. She picked out a shimmering stone and turned it over in her fingers.

"A purple amethyst!" whispered Jaminta. "Good choice, Clarabel."

"And now, Your Royal Highnesses," said the empress, "we will have a short break while the treasure is taken inside. Everyone will meet at the harbor in one hour, and then the boat races will begin!"

CHAPTER THIRTEEN

A Princess Team

The princesses rushed inside to get ready for the Royal Regatta. Clarabel asked if they were allowed to take a rowboat out on the ocean to watch the race close-up.

"As long as you're very careful," said the queen of Winteria, her blue eyes serious. "It's really hard work rowing those little boats, even on a calm sea. I don't think you realize how tricky it can be."

"Yes, Your Majesty. We'll be careful," said the princesses, trying not to giggle.

"If only they'd seen us in that storm," Lulu said after the queen had gone.

"It's a good thing they didn't!" Clarabel laughed.

Because the Royal Regatta was such an important occasion, the girls put on beautiful dresses and their favorite tiaras.

Clarabel's dress was pale blue and her hair shone like gold. Her tiara was decorated with sparkling sapphires, and on her wrist she wore the sapphire bracelet with the single pearl that had healed the dolphin. The purple amethyst from the treasure chest was stored safely in her jewelry box.

"Ready?" asked Emily, swishing her pink silk dress. On top of her red curls rested a tiara made to look like golden leaves.

“I am!” Lulu somersaulted past in her yellow dress, holding her gold crown in one hand.

Jaminta nodded. She looked beautiful in a dark-green dress and a tiara sparkling with Onica crystals.

Laughing so hard they almost fell over, the princesses raced down the hill to the harbor to find the boat.

Clarabel reached the little rowboat last and stopped, breathless. Jaminta untied the rope and the girls climbed in and picked up the oars.

Lulu ran along the narrow harbor wall with the sea far below her. Then she flipped head over heels onto the jetty before climbing into the boat.

Clarabel dipped her oar into the water as the boat began to move. "I wish I could do all that." She sighed. "But I'm just not good at that kind of thing."

"What kind of thing?" said Emily.

Clarabel chewed her lip. "You know, climbing and acrobatics, like the somersault Lulu just did. All the skills you need to rescue animals. I don't think I'll ever be very good. I wish I could help more."

Lulu put down her oar and stared at Clarabel in astonishment. "Clarabel, I think you must be the silliest princess alive," she said, shaking her head.

Clarabel's eyes widened.

"Who got into the sea in the middle of the storm to help the dolphin?" asked Lulu.

"I did," said Clarabel. "But —"

"Who could hear him calling by listening to the pearl?" said Jaminta. "If you hadn't been there, we wouldn't have found him."

"You can understand animals," said Emily. "That's an amazing talent!"

"Squawk!" The little blue parrot flew down from the harbor wall and landed on Clarabel's shoulder, eyeing her beadily.

Clarabel grinned and stroked the parrot's feathers. "I guess you're right."

"Climbing and somersaults are only part of it," said Emily. "We all have different gifts. That's why we make such a good team."

"And I'll teach you the somersaults," added Lulu, her eyes gleaming. Clarabel had to laugh.

Rowing hard, they left the harbor for the calm blue ocean beyond. In the distance, the white sails of the racing boats whisked across the water.

Four magical rings gleamed on the princesses' fingers: one ruby, one sapphire, one emerald, and one topaz.

The girls linked arms and settled down to watch the boat race, knowing that whatever adventure came along, they would always be the Rescue Princesses.